For Luke & all of my students who know
me as Ms. Warren or Mrs. Townsend

Alma & the Worry Stone

Written by Sara Townsend
Illustrated by Hannah Teakle

It was the first day of school.
The sun was shining and the sky was
glowing, but Alma was not excited.

She was filled with worry from her
head to her toes and her insides
were not delighted.

On the walk to school Alma's mother
noticed something didn't seem right.

Alma was quiet, her fingers were sweaty,
and her face was filled with fright.

"What's the matter my darling dear?"
Asked her mother.
"I can tell you're not feeling yourself."

"I'm worried I won't make any friends"
said Alma.
"and I'll have to play all by myself."

"What if my teacher doesn't like me
and I do nothing but work all day?

What if we have to count to one million
and THEN have to write an essay?"

"What if I'm given a magic bean and it turns me invisible so I can't be seen?"

"What if a dragon comes and breaks down our door? Then I'd get left behind because I couldn't be seen anymore!"

"Alma, my dear, rest your worries of fear,
for you have all the power here!

When your worried thoughts make you
feel alone, just reach into your pocket
and pull out your worry stone!"

"Close your eyes and imagine good thoughts
or memories that you've had once before.

Your good thoughts will battle your bad
thoughts and slay them to the floor!"

"You're going to be fine, you're not on
your own. When you have your worry stone,
you're never alone.

Your day will go great, you'll know just
what to do. Pull out your worry stone if
a worry comes true."

So Alma walked to her classroom
with confidence and grace.

And there stood her teacher, with
the biggest smile on her face!

Alma's teacher was kind
and wasn't scary at all!

Instead of writing essays, they
played with a question ball!

Soon after, the librarian paid them
a visit. She brought so many books,
there was no reading limit!

The class was given time to read
and explore. And Alma found a book
about dragon folklore!

Before Alma knew it, it was time to go.
Wait a minute, a new worry started to GROW!

Alma didn't want to go home at the end of
the day. She loved her new class so much
and really wanted to stay.

She started to worry about all of the
fun she could miss.

So she pulled out her stone, closed her eyes,
and made a mental list.

Alma started reciting things that made
her happy throughout the day.

By thinking of all the happy thoughts,
her bad ones went away.

Alma grabbed her bag and waved
good-bye as she went to see her mom.

She held onto her worry stone
and it made her feel calm!

"See it wasn't so bad,
I knew it wouldn't be."

"You have to learn how to tame your dragons...
Who knew it would be this easy?"

Take Control
of Your Worries
and fears!

Be brave and tame your dragons
like Alma did here!

Made in the USA
Las Vegas, NV
14 August 2023

76080177R00021